DISNEY'S
TOONTOWN

The
Substitooth
Fairy

Written by Margaret Snyder

Illustrated by Judith Clarke and Peter Emslie

MERRIGOLD PRESS • NEW YORK

©1995 The Walt Disney Company. All rights reserved. Printed in the U.S.A. No part of
this book may be reproduced or copied in any form without written permission from the
copyright owner. MERRIGOLD PRESS® and MERRIGOLD PRESS & DESIGN™
are the property of Merrigold Press, New York, New York 10022. Library of Congress
Catalog Card Number: 94-78273   ISBN: 0-307-11181-4 A MCMXCV

Daisy Duck was getting ready for bed when she suddenly heard a **THUD!** against her window. "What was that?" she whispered. She tiptoed over to the window, slowly moved the curtain aside, and peeked out.

There, in the flower box below her window, was Tooth Fairy. She was untangling herself from the petunias as she shook her finger at her wand. "This is ridiculous!" Tooth Fairy scolded. "You're too new to be acting up!"

The wand blushed and sputtered.

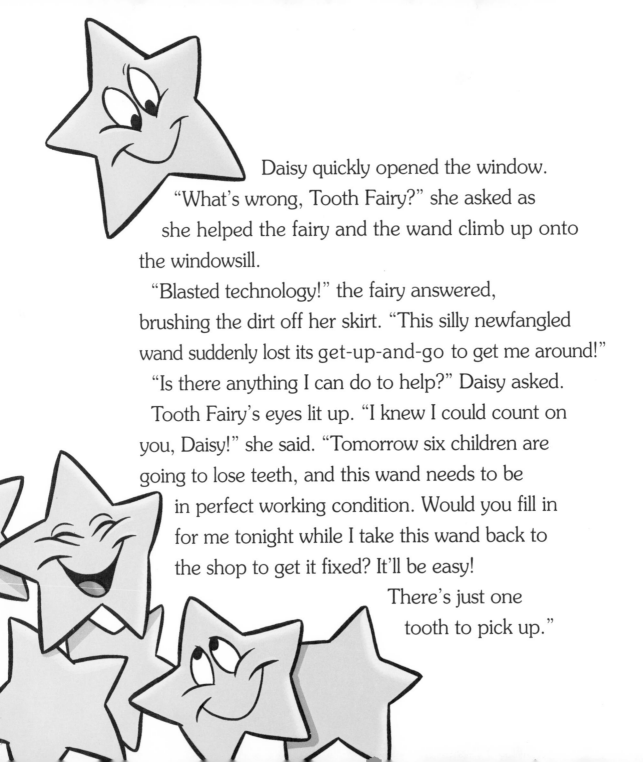

Daisy quickly opened the window.

"What's wrong, Tooth Fairy?" she asked as she helped the fairy and the wand climb up onto the windowsill.

"Blasted technology!" the fairy answered, brushing the dirt off her skirt. "This silly newfangled wand suddenly lost its get-up-and-go to get me around!"

"Is there anything I can do to help?" Daisy asked.

Tooth Fairy's eyes lit up. "I knew I could count on you, Daisy!" she said. "Tomorrow six children are going to lose teeth, and this wand needs to be in perfect working condition. Would you fill in for me tonight while I take this wand back to the shop to get it fixed? It'll be easy! There's just one tooth to pick up."

Daisy was stunned. "Fill in for you?"
she asked. "How could I ever do that?"
Tooth Fairy handed Daisy two pouches.
"All you have to do is find the tooth under
the pillow and put it in this pouch. Then
take a coin from the other pouch and put it
under the pillow. Pillow, pouch, pouch, pillow.
You don't have to be a fairy to do that!"

"But how will I fly through all those windows?"
Daisy stammered.

"Here, take my old backup wand," Tooth Fairy
said. "It still has some sparks left–I think."
Tooth Fairy looked down at her watch and gasped.
"Time to go!" she said. Then she stared sternly
at her wand. "Don't drop me in another flower
box," she warned, and trailing fairy dust, she
flew out into the night sky.

Daisy waved good-bye to the fairy. "Oh, no!" she suddenly exclaimed. "I forgot to ask whose tooth I'm supposed to pick up!"

The old wand sputtered and pointed at Daisy's pillow as if it were trying to tell her something.

"I'm not going to bed," Daisy said. The wand pointed again. This time Daisy understood. "Oh! I should check under every child's pillow in Toontown until I find the tooth! What a grand idea! Now carry me out to the window!" Daisy shouted, pointing the wand. The wand yawned. It was tired from the explanation and needed to recharge.

"Oh, brother," Daisy said. "I guess I'll have to walk to the first house!"

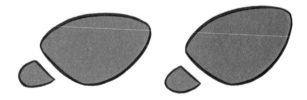

By the time Daisy got there, the wand
was in much better shape. "Ready?"
Daisy asked. The wand winked and carried
Daisy a little unsteadily up through the window and
into a little girl's bedroom. But as Daisy hovered
over the little girl's bed, the wand began to crackle
and Daisy dropped with a **THUD!**

"Mommy! There's a monster in my room!" the
little girl screamed. Daisy scrambled to her feet
and headed for the window. Then she remembered
to check for the tooth. She raced back to the bed,
picked up the pillow, and peeked underneath.
There was no tooth. "Go back to sleep,
honey!" Daisy whispered to the little girl.
"It's only a dream."

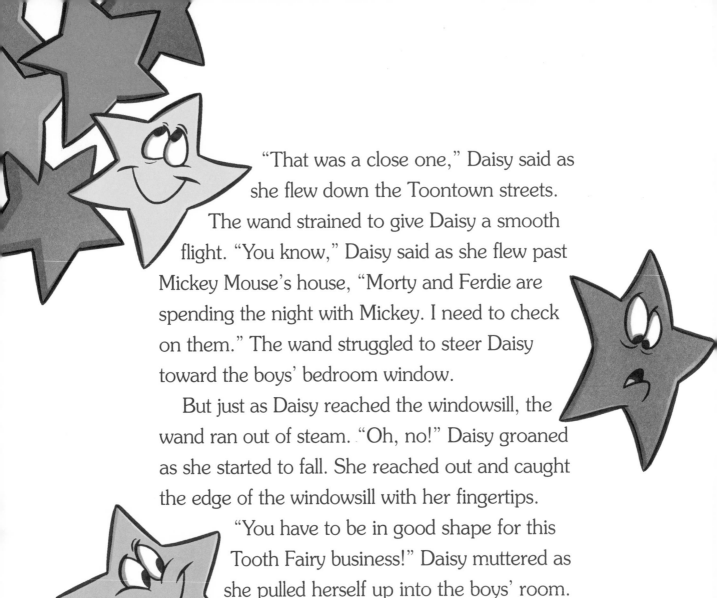

"That was a close one," Daisy said as she flew down the Toontown streets. The wand strained to give Daisy a smooth flight. "You know," Daisy said as she flew past Mickey Mouse's house, "Morty and Ferdie are spending the night with Mickey. I need to check on them." The wand struggled to steer Daisy toward the boys' bedroom window.

But just as Daisy reached the windowsill, the wand ran out of steam. "Oh, no!" Daisy groaned as she started to fall. She reached out and caught the edge of the windowsill with her fingertips.

"You have to be in good shape for this Tooth Fairy business!" Daisy muttered as she pulled herself up into the boys' room.

Daisy checked Morty and Ferdie's pillows and came up empty-handed. "Onward!" a determined Daisy said to the wand. The wand sighed as it carried Daisy into the night. With each trip in and out of a child's bedroom window, it lost more zip. Sometimes Daisy made it through the bedroom window, and other times she landed in a flower box or in a tree.

"I've got to find that tooth," Daisy said. "I'm running out of pillows to check!"

Finally
Daisy flew
over to Donald's house to check on Huey,
Dewey, and Louie. She was about to fly
into their bedroom when she heard giggling.
Daisy peered into the window and saw the
boys in the midst of a pillow fight. "Still up
at this hour!" Daisy gasped. "We're
going to have to come back later,"
she told the wand. And Daisy flew
away before the boys could see her.

"Let's find a place to rest,"
Daisy suggested, "and I'll try to remember
all of my stops."

The wand looked relieved. But just as it was
about to deposit Daisy on a bench near the
Fireworks Factory, it completely lost its power!

"Oh, no!" Daisy said as she looked down.
"Not here!" And with a crash she landed on the
plunger for the Fireworks Factory!

BOOM!

Fireworks flashed in the night. "This will
wake all of Toontown!" Daisy cried.

Daisy was right.
She watched
Mickey, Minnie, Donald,
Huey, Dewey, Louie, and the other
Toontown residents come running outside
in their pajamas to see the spectacle.

"Now what do I do?" Daisy asked the wand. The
wand looked hopeful and pointed to the crowd.
"I can't go over there," Daisy said. "I still have
to find that tooth!" The wand smiled and again
pointed to the crowd. This time Daisy noticed the
wand was pointing straight at Huey, Dewey, and
Louie. "That's it!" Daisy shouted. "Now's my
chance to check under their pillows."

Daisy raced to Donald's house. She pointed the wand at the window, and with one final burst of magic, it carried her into the boys' room. Quickly she checked under Huey's pillow. No tooth. She checked under Dewey's pillow. Still no tooth. She checked under Louie's pillow. There was the tooth!

Daisy scooped up the tooth and replaced it with a shiny new coin. "We did it!" she said to the wand. Then Daisy tucked the wand under her arm, went downstairs, and sneaked outside. Nobody noticed her as she headed home.

A very tired Daisy climbed
the stairs to her bedroom.
Tooth Fairy was waiting for her.
"How did it go, Daisy?" she asked.
Daisy handed the fairy the pouches and
sighed. "Well, let's just say it was a blast!"
Tooth Fairy looked confused. "What do you
mean?" she asked.
Daisy just smiled. She had never
been so happy to see her own pillow.